To my hero, Gabe, who is never afraid to fall down
and get up again. You are courage.
—S.V.

To Purnell "Nell" Sabky, who taught us love,
courage and resilience, and the power of community.
—P.H.R.

The illustrations in this book were created using traditional and digital inks, gouache, watercolor, and tea.

Cataloging-in-Publication Data has been applied for and
may be obtained from the Library of Congress.

ISBN 978-1-4197-4646-8

Text copyright © 2021 Susan Verde
Illustrations copyright © 2021 Peter H. Reynolds
Reynolds Studio assistance by Julia Young Cuffe
Book design by Pamela Notarantonio and Jade Rector

Printed and bound in U.S.A.
10 9 8 7 6 5 4 3 2 1

Abrams Books for Young Readers are available at special discounts when purchased in quantity for
premiums and promotions as well as fundraising or educational use. Special editions can also be
created to specification. For details, contact specialsales@abramsbooks.com or the address below.

ABRAMS The Art of Books
195 Broadway, New York, NY 10007
abramsbooks.com

I AM COURAGE

A BOOK of RESILIENCE

BY SUSAN VERDE · ART BY PETER H. REYNOLDS

Abrams Books for Young Readers · New York

When my mind tells me "I can't."

I look inside myself and find
the strength that lives deep down,

and I tell my mind

"Yes, I CAN!"

I am courage.

I can trust what my gut is telling me.
I believe in myself.

I can feel scared but still carry on.
I persevere.

I can tumble and still get up again.
I am resilient.

I can lean on those around me.
I am not afraid to ask for support.

I can encourage another
when there is doubt.
I am uplifting.

I can know there is no shame
in sharing. I tell my story.

I can step in when others are struggling.
I know how to help.

I can be the one to clear the way for someone else.
I am an example.

When I feel uncertain and start
to lose my balance,

I find my center
and gather my strength.

I know what I am.

I am
courage.

And I can keep going.

We are strong.
We are capable.
We are important.

We are courage.

And we are
triumphant.

Author's Note

Often when we think of someone brave, we think of one who is without fear, boldly slaying dragons or moving through the world conquering every obstacle in their way. It may look on the outside like things come easy for some, that they are never afraid. But that isn't what's true. Although what scares each of us may be different, fear is something we *all* feel, and we don't need to hide it. It is okay to talk about. Bravery isn't fearlessness; real courage comes from being afraid and still facing what challenges you, whether that means asking for help, sharing your truth, or slaying a dragon. Once you rule out danger, fear is a place for opportunity and growth. *I Am Courage* is a story about how to find courage within ourselves when we feel afraid or unable. It's about the ways in which we are brave every day—and how we *will* fall down, but we all have the ability to get back up again and keep on going. We are all courageous.

As kids are learning to be and love who they are in the world and to find their voices and their resilience, yoga and mindfulness practices offer many ways to help them build courage in a safe and noncompetitive space. Yoga allows us to approach things that challenge us with curiosity and kindness to ourselves. It gives us a chance to observe our fear and to recognize if there is real danger, or if we can keep going. There are poses that are difficult, and we might fall every time we try them; there are also poses that are powerful and give us a way to express our inner strength. Being brave in yoga carries over into our everyday lives. Yoga releases chemicals in our brains that lower feelings of fear and stress, it strengthens our sense of capability, and by nature of trying something difficult, helps us to face challenges *off* the mat, too. We can take these courageous feelings out into the world.

Mindfulness is also about cultivating an awareness of our fear and learning to create distance from it instead of getting lost in it. You can do this very simply by focusing on your breath. Anchoring your mind to the rhythm of your breath during times of fear can give you a moment to pause, relax, make decisions, and see things more clearly—making it easier to keep going or to stop in the face of real danger.

Following are a few special yoga poses and breathing techniques to help you feel confident and brave and to keep being the courageous human that you are!

Fierce Pose: This is a great pose for strengthening your legs and core while using your imagination. Sometimes it's also called Chair pose or even Rocket Ship pose. Stand tall with your feet together. Bend your knees, pressing into your heels, and bring your arms up overhead or as high as you can. You will feel this pose in your whole body. It's a challenge to stay in it, so focus on breathing in and out through your nose as you slowly count to ten. Maybe imagine you are about to bravely take off into space. You are FIERCE!

Warrior 3 Pose: The Warrior poses are great confidence boosters and can make you feel strong, but this one in particular challenges balance and focus to make you feel incredibly courageous. Stand tall with your feet together. Reach your arms straight over your head, pressing your palms together. Bending at the waist, lift one leg straight behind you as you reach your arms forward, until your arms, head, and lifted leg are on the

same horizontal plane, like the letter *T*. Make sure both hips face down and your back is flat. Let your eyes find a spot on the mat or floor, and breathe through your nose. See how long you can stay balanced. Feel the strength in your whole body as it works to keep you in this pose. After a few slow, deep breaths, return to standing with your arms relaxed by your sides. When you are ready, try the other leg. See which side feels more challenging. Notice how powerful you feel.

Lion's Breath: Who is more courageous than a mighty lion? This is an awesome way to let go of fear and anxiety and feel brave by letting out *your* inner lion. Kneel down on the ground and sit back on your ankles. Rest your palms on your thighs and take a deep breath in through your nose as you push your hands into your legs. Then as you breathe out, let your hands relax, stick out your tongue, and let out a loud sound like you are roaring your biggest roar! It may feel silly at first, but after a few rounds of this you will feel stronger and more energized, as if you are letting go of what scares you with each roar.

Even Breathing: This mindful breathing activity allows you to find balance in your mind and body. When we are afraid, our hearts beat quickly, and our breathing becomes shallow as if we are gulping for air; steady breathing allows us to slow things down and gives us a place to focus our attention away from fear. Sit up in a comfortable position or lie down on your back. Close your eyes. Place your hands on your belly and begin noticing your breath as you breathe in and out through your nose. Then add a count to your breath, purposely slowing it down. Start by breathing in for a count of three and breathing out for a count of three. When you are feeling comfortable, add a second or two to your count. You could end up counting to six or more on both the in breath and the out breath; just keep both counts the same. Do this for a few rounds and feel yourself begin to settle and relax. If your mind wanders and you lose count, don't worry, just start again. When you have finished, make sure you open your eyes slowly, taking a moment to notice how you feel before jumping back into your day.

Don't forget to remind yourself: You've got this! I know that you do, because you are courage.